THE 304 MONSTERS OF WEST VIRGINIA

CATALOGED MONSTERS 1-104

VERONICA CARTER

WITH

STEPHEN BIAS

The Henio Press

NOTES

304 Monsters, there are always 304.

If you get lucky and kill one, another will take its place. It's part of the curse. I still wonder about the whole West Virginia area code being the same. Did someone at the phone company know in 1947 everything happening here? Anyone who'd have that answer is long gone. I've tried to meet with the governor, but he refuses to see me.

I'm dead if you find this journal at Wally's house and got in with the door code. These are personal notes of the monsters I know of and have encountered. When I jot this down (Jan 2025), I have taken the 81 that Wally had extensive background on and added a few to get to 104.

If you have no idea who I am, who Jennifer is, or what I am talking about. Walk away, leave the stuff you've found along with this notebook, and never look back. Most of the trinkets you see here aren't worth much, and it's better you never know the truth about this place.

I do want it known that Jennifer came up with the names, which I think are ridiculous, and I can't believe I am writing some of this down. If she's with you and the reason you found my notes, please tell her that I still think these names are awful and she should be ashamed.

A star indicates that I've taken care of the creature, and it is no longer living. I was going to list them by county, but that was way too much work. Underneath this journal are several folders of news clippings, drawings, and testimonies for most of these. I tried to keep them in the numbers I have ordered here. Ghosts are not included except for the three I know who actively kill.

Nothing*

Taken care of, but one of the most frightening things a person can encounter. I'm worried about what will take its place. This demon from hell that took my best friend's life, her father, and an 11-year-old boy. We have no idea how many bodies we can lay at its feet. Completely invisible and insanely powerful, it took pleasure in murder and despair. Jennifer told me he was dragged back to hell. I hope he rots there.

THE WITCHES OF WEIRTON

ARABELLA

THIS WILL TAKE listings two to ten, a coven of witches that now reside in Weirton. Led by Arabella, who I have found records dating all the way back to 1871. She is very powerful and evil. They range from harmless to the ones that revel in chaos and destruction. Arabella has a deep-seated hatred for this place and its inhabitants. However she exercises restraint nowadays, but there have been moments throughout this state's history where she has done some pretty vile things.

(Added March 2025) We are currently in a truce because I have agreed to help in the search for #75.

THE WITCHES OF
WEIRTON

BABETTE OR AUNT BABBY

HIPPY, who was friendly when I first met her. I've run into her a couple of times since. I don't think she likes to hurt people. She seems to be only concerned with the protection of her own.

THE WITCHES OF
WEIRTON

ARIEL

MUSCLE-BOUND GOTH WITCH (YES, that's a thing)
Hate her, confrontational and always itching for a
fight. I think she's dangerous; if she ever gets control of this family, she will bathe the state in blood.
Mind control seems to be her gift. She gets people
to do her dirty work for her.

THE WITCHES OF WEIRTON

LYNN

LOOKS like what people envision when they think of witches. Moles, black hair, cackling laugh the whole nine yards. A skilled potion maker and a master at whipping up poisons.

THE WITCHES OF WEIRTON

EMMA

NEVER MET HER, only know she exists. She's never with the family. She's usually away for some reason. (Maybe she hates them? Or maybe they had a falling out of some sort?)

THE WITCHES OF
WEIRTON

ELLA

THIS ONE WEARS a mask for some reason. It looks like twigs glued together with only her eyes visible by cut out. It covers her whole face. Is she disfigured or something else?

THE WITCHES OF
WEIRTON
TRISHA

THIS IDIOT DRESSES like the character Tinkerbell with wings and a short sparkly dress. She talks like she's been eating mushrooms for days. I'm not afraid of this one in the slightest.

The Witches of Weirton
Minne

SPEAKS IN RHYME, which pisses me off. It's not cute, it's not creative, it's annoying.

The Witches of Weirton

Grace

A 15-year-old girl and the youngest of the coven, she might be the most powerful, too. I saved her when she was a child. She felt like she owed me. Maybe I can reason with her?

MOTHMAN

AH YES, the Mothman. Chicago and New Jersey people are full of shit and looking for attention. She never left the Mountain State. She only appears in front of someone because they are near her eggs, and she sees them as a threat.

THE BROTHERS
FERGUSON
GABE

THE NEXT THREE are the triplets. Their mother died before an emergency c-section was performed to remove them. They are undead and look nothing alike. They feed on human flesh. Gabe is extremely sensible and highly intelligent. He can be reasoned with and is only looking to survive.

THE BROTHERS FERGUSON

SAWYER

THIS ONE HATES what he is and is very emotional about the situation. Gabe keeps him in line, but Sawyer always seeks the cure. I wonder who took care of these three as babies and then turned them loose on the world.

THE BROTHERS FERGUSON

OWEN

THE MEAN ONE of the bunch. I tried to kill him, but bullets and fire didn't work. This one takes pride in what he is and gorges on people. The brothers are close, and I don't think the other two will take kindly to me offing one of their own if I even can.

BRIAR OF THE
GREENBRIER

DEEP in the woods of Greenbrier County is a briar patch. If you get entangled, you are slowly consumed. I am curious to know if the area is sentient.

Bob

I do not know if this is his name, but I call him that. I love Bob. He's adorable. He can't speak and communicates through grunts. He's 7 feet 5 inches at least and covered in thick brown hair. I am pretty sure people who have seen him claim this is bigfoot. He is out in Mullens near Twin Falls, and I get excited when I see him. Just don't make him angry. He doesn't know his strength.

DEPRESSING DON

I THINK 17 and 18 are connected. I just can't prove it, but I must stop both immediately. Every six months or so, Don (Unsure of his actual name. Jennifer calls him this. I don't get the reference.) goes on a date with a woman. That woman then commits suicide shortly after. I have a video of Don and his last victim. All he does is talk while they eat. He pays for the dinner, kisses their cheek, and leaves them sitting there. These women show no signs of mental illness or depression. They go after the meal and kill themselves in a variety of ways. Is this a power of suggestion thing?

The Man Who Wasn't There

This is not the same man as 17. I've gotten a sketch artist to draw him. The picture should be underneath this journal in the folder. At least, I am confident they aren't the same person. Again, it is the state of West Virginia, so you can't be too confident. I just can't shake the feeling they are in the same vein.

Women all over the state report meeting an attractive man who sweeps them off their feet. He weds them, they get a home together and try for a baby. Once they are impregnated, The woman awakes one morning to discover he has disappeared, vanished without a trace.

There are no photos, banking records, no proof of his existence anywhere. There are no signs of him anywhere. The dangerous thing in these situations is that no one besides the woman affected can remember the man. People think the women claiming to know him have lost their minds. I've gotten DNA on seven of the children. They are fathered by the same man. I need to solve this one quickly.

FloraKate

KATE LIVES in a concrete basement in Huntington. She gives off a scent that causes people to lose their inhibitions. I've been told it resembles an orchid with a hint of lemon. Once someone inhales the pheromones, they can't control themselves. It's random, also. One person might confess their sins and cry uncontrollably; another may strip naked and lie on the floor rubbing their nipples. I hate the name Jennifer has come up with for her. I've spoken to Kate in her bubble. That's no way to live.

SNARL

A BLACK BEAR from the woods in Prichard. Wayne County has a lot of woodlands and houses spaced out, so he stays hidden. Snarl can speak, and not in a loveable way like Baloo. He's vulgar, and not only that, he's big, on the higher end of size for a black bear. The son of a bitch called me a cunt the first time we met. If you need anything from him, take Snarl Little Debbie products. It's the only thing he seems to have a soft spot for.

BACKMASK BEAUTY

A VINYL RECORD from the 1980s; I doubt it's older than that. I hope there is only one in existence. It is a bluegrass album with various satanic imagery on the cover. The painting is of a scantily clad woman, her hair teased in typical fashion for the time, hanging on the devil with a banjo in her hand. The title is "Satan's Smile and the Wiggle Wiggle." I have no idea if there is any meaning behind that. There are no track listings on the back, just a tease to 'Not Play The Album Backwards.' People who don't heed the warning are found dead, their brains literally melted and pouring from their noses. I have to find this before some idiot puts it on CD or, God forbid, somehow uploads it to the internet.

S.T.P.D.

A PARASITE that enters the host through sexual transmission and begins feeding on them. It takes complete control as it eats away at their organs and muscles. The process takes about a year before finding someone to mate with at a dive bar. An extraordinary fact is that the host doesn't eat food after infection. They only consume alcohol. Maybe I can use that to my advantage?

LADYFISH

CAN'T CALL IT A MERMAID. In Summersville Lake is a half woman, half fish. It leans more heavily on the fish side. It's mindless and an eating machine. Usually, she doesn't bother people unless her caretaker (Craig, I hate that guy.) forgets to feed her. Craig is paid out of pocket by a senator's office. Meaning people up in Washington know of this state's plight.

Horndog

PRECISELY, as Jennifer named it. A coyote with what looks like a unicorn horn. It's the stupidest thing I've seen yet. I think it may just be some form of cancer or something. It doesn't exhibit anything special. However, the people of Dobbin seem to worship it. Maybe I need to take a closer look.

NADINE*

CURSED BY WALLY IN 1972, Nadine was an arrogant young lady who cared only about appearances. She would age at an alarming rate, but to combat it, she would have to feed on someone's essence. As she kissed them, they would age while she would grow younger. As of 2023, she had killed over 600 men. She was quite possibly the most prolific serial killer in history.

SHAMAN

JENNIFER and I are in total agreement. Chief Cornstalk cursed this land in 1777, which is why West Virginia is the way it is today. He uttered it at Fort Randolph after soldiers murdered his son. Every year since then, on the winter solstice, a prominent hooded native american shaman murders someone inside the state's borders. The person is always random, and Shaman will not stop until it kills them. The governor and several local FBI offices are aware of this. It is covered up every year.

It skins the person alive and can not be hurt. Doctor Herschel Jeffery at West Virginia University is an expert on the matter and has seen Shaman four times. He is trying as hard as I am to stop it. I write this in October of 2025, and I am dreading December.

DINER DAME

A DINER in the town of Logan burnt to the ground after a robbery. The waitress was assaulted and left to die. (I wonder if she knew her assailants.) This is the first ghost on the list, but she is no ordinary spirit. The diner randomly appears on a lonely road in Logan like nothing is wrong. Anyone who enters is found burnt to a crisp in the same spot the following day. It last appeared in 2021.

COOKIE

HE TIES IN WITH 27. When the diner burnt, he was there, a cook who tried to get her out and failed. I tried to find history on him and can't. Something is really off about him. Police reports from the 50s say he was weird and scared people. Is he the cause of the diner appearing and disappearing? I am going to investigate when I get the time.

THE CAMDEN
MENACE

WHEN CAMDEN PARK closes for the night, they do a terrible job cleaning the park, and I now know why. There is a small creature that lives out by the log flume. It's toddler-sized, with eyes that take up over half its head, pointed ears, and long, sharp teeth. It eats the food off the ground and in the trash cans. Its favorite is obviously the Pronto Pup. I've seen the footage. It's pretty frightening looking. However, it hides from people and supposedly has been there since 1982. It hides when confronted, so I don't see it as a threat.

Virgin Marty

Martin Sloan, a Wheeling, West Virginia resident, and a disgusting man. He's overweight, unshaven, and talks while always stuffed with snot. I've never seen him bathed, and he smells. He spends all day on the internet looking at porn. Marty's gift is he can remove his body parts, and they can function without being a part of the whole. For example, he can remove his eye, and it can roll places. He has done this peeping on people. I've warned him.

HIVE

IN A LOVELY WOODED area of Chester is a humanoid-type figure made up of insects. There are various creepy crawlers, roaches, lighting bugs, beetles, stink bugs, mosquitoes, and many others. But no spiders, thank God. It has killed before but keeps to itself. It won't harm children. Several have stumbled upon it. It's not a top priority.

WOOD WHISPERER

I HAD no idea what the hell this was talking about when I first read it in Nora's notes. It kept mentioning Elklick. That is the original name for the town of Elk. Out in the woods is a covered-over trail that, when some people travel, they will hear a voice whispering to them. Once they leave, the voice continues to speak to them. Eventually, they are driven mad and institutionalized. What frightens me most is if you talk to one of the nine people afflicted so far, they tell you the same thing: I await the day of reckoning. I am scared it is building an army or something worse.

WOLVES OF WOOD COUNTY

LARRY

A FAMILY of werewolves from northwest West Virginia. Werewolves are harmless. They don't turn into the hulking beasts you think they do. They turn into typical wolves and are usually shot on someone's land or get hit on the interstate. The oldest brother in the group and the least friendly.

Wolves of Wood County

Dallas

DALLAS SITS on a porch and smokes cigarettes all day. I don't even think he changes anymore.

WOLVES OF WOOD COUNTY

ROGER

THE WISEST OF THE BUNCH, and has helped me locate some unsavory characters. Decent fellow and adores the family. He might be my favorite of the bunch.

Wolves of Wood County

David

DAVID IS a little too into the one with nature rhetoric. He's a good carpenter, though, and built the family homes in their holler. He has two children whom I've never met. I don't think either resides in this state.

Wolves of Wood County

County

Ronnie

Something happened with Ronnie, and he left the family to branch out on his own. Rumor swirls that it was due to an argument with the youngest brother.

WOLVES OF WOOD COUNTY

STEVE

THE YOUNGEST AND the only other one with children, his offspring don't seem affected by lycanthropy. One of his daughters has a teen girl, and she's a handful. She tried to fist-fight me twice. The family sticks to themselves and leaves everyone alone. I wish there were more like this.

Rag Doll

I HAVE SEEN this doll before. It was in Grace's room back in 2013. A dirty, patched-up rag doll that looks like something from the early 1940s or late 1930s. It has brown yarn for hair and is missing one button eye. The toy is stained and looks worn. If someone keeps the doll, it eventually traps their soul inside it. The victim shows all the signs of a massive stroke. If you put the item up to your ear, you can hear the people trapped inside crying to get out. I have no idea of its location.

FAWNY

A BEAUTIFUL DOE that when you stumble upon it, its mouth opens four ways, and a giant tongue fires out, spawning several feet. It wraps around the individual's neck and cuts off their air supply. Once the prey is weakened, it draws them in and stomps on the person with its hooves until they can be consumed easier as a paste.

BUCKY *

THE MATE OF FAWNY, with similar tactics. I got him outside of Moundsville. He had killed two local hunters. It took three days to track him, and with broadhead tip arrows, I was able to take him down from above. Bucky was a gorgeous 10-point buck if you remove the fact that its mouth and throat were lined with over 300 razor-sharp teeth. Its head is on the wall in Wally's old living room.

MR. MORROW

THE COVERED bridge in Milton has existed for decades, even being moved, torn down, and rebuilt. The first case of Mr. Morrow was in 1965. A couple out for a stroll was by the covered bridge when a thin man gave chase. They claimed he looked unnatural, wearing suspenders, a straw hat, and barefoot. The thing that unnerved them was his grin looked to be too large for his face.

He told them he was going to get them, and as they ran, they crossed the cover bridge, only to emerge on the other side in 1975, not aging a day, and people giving them up for dead. It happened again that same year. A couple was chased through the bridge, and it's a repeated cycle every ten years after that. I'll be there in November when the couple from 2015 comes through. I hope I get a look at Mr. Morrow.

CHILD OF
CHEAT LAKE

PEOPLE WHO DROWN in Cheat Lake might have been victims of an underwater creature. It looks like a small child reaching out from under the water. People dive in, trying to be heroic, and are grabbed. The face of the child melts away to what can only be described as a skeleton with human eyes. I have spoken to a survivor. Max Adkins escaped because of their prosthetic arm coming loose.

Thurmond
Twosome
One

THERE IS a sealed-up mine in the abandoned mining town of Thurmond. The town became a tourist attraction, but no one is allowed in the mine. Only five or six residents are there, so I don't have to worry about the locals. Thurmond isn't a problem because only five people live there. Two men struck something down in the mines in 1930, and it mutated them somehow.

THURMOND
TWOSOME
Two

EYEWITNESS THAT HAVE ENCOUNTERED the pair say they are covered in coal dust from eating it, their eyes glow a bright white (Nocturnal?), and it looks like their bones have continued to grow out of their skin at the joints. They are dangerous and feral. They aren't a priority since they can't leave the mine.

FEAST

I'VE ENCOUNTERED this being before, and it is the one I am terrified of. I don't know if they can form one giant spider the size of a car or a thousand little ones. I've seen this entity in several configurations when it would go into the basement to exact revenge on Wally. Imagine my surprise to find out Wally wasn't its only meal. I've got tons of documents here of them in every corner of West Virginia dishing punishment to those who play with forces they shouldn't. Sometimes, it's best to leave things alone.

SHIFTY

THE CLASSIC SHAPESHIFTER, this man, woman, or whatever can assume anyone's appearance and voice. It typically mimics the recently deceased. However, I have no record of it killing someone itself. It usually takes possessions or robs people. There haven't been any reports of violent crimes. The MO has remained unchanged since 1905. This sucker is old and a creature of habit. It's another on the list, but is not a concern for now.

Fuck Tar

High up in Holly River State Park, out where the forest is densest, is a set of pine trees that leak sap. This gooey substance, when touched, stimulates the LSt cells in the spinal cord, causing an orgasm. That doesn't sound bad until you realize it continues to affect you until your nervous system shuts down and your heart gives out. A specialist cut down the trees, but now the ones 10 feet away exhibit the same behavior.

CARETAKER

I HAVE no problems with Franklin. He is currently the caretaker at Mount Wood Cementary in Wheeling. He tends to the grounds, buries the dead, and when no one is looking late at night, he digs a body up and consumes it. He doesn't take any of their jewelry or items and cries when he does it. He's never explained why he has to do it; it's just that things would be catastrophic if he didn't. During our talks, he slipped up and told me he's been doing this since the late 1700s. I started going through records, and I believe he was at Fort Rudolph, but I can't be sure. Did the incident with Cornstalk have something to do with his condition?

The Orange Wall

The Kenova Pumpkin House is a staple of Halloween in the Mountain State, and I would make the trip down to see it every year. I had no idea that the truth of it was so depressing. In 1976, a young boy named Geno went missing after Halloween night. He was dressed as a pirate and had gone out trick or treating alone at eight years old. (It was the 70s) He was found 25 miles away, strangled and naked. He wasn't a very nice boy and was known to be a hoodlum. His biggest prank was stealing pumpkins from people's porches during Halloween and smashing them.

I can't call him a spirit because on October 29th every year, he is seen looking admirably at the house for the evening before disappearing. I don't think he is a ghost because everyone can see him in his pirate costume and all. In 1977, when there were no pumpkins, Geno somehow violently strangled a young trick-or-treater named Ellie. I think the pumpkins keep him at bay somehow, and everyone in Kenova knows it. I'll find out soon enough be-cause he's next on my list.

The Dusk Akers Family

Grover

A FAMILY of vampires and a caricature of what people think of residents of this state. They hail from a town called Dusk in Gilmer County until I started hunting them. I've killed two, but my work is far from done. Inbred and vicious, and stupid as they are cruel. The whole state will be better off once I kill every last one of them. Grover is the "Pa" of the group.

THE DUSK AKERS FAMILY

FEBBIE

THE FAMILY MATRIARCH and the eldest. I don't know if she birthed the younger ones on the list, but I know they call her Ma.

THE DUSK AKERS
FAMILY
HARLAN

MOST OF THE family takes orders from him. He, along with #58, is the one who hunts for food.

THE DUSK AKERS FAMILY

STELLA

I took Stella's arm in Matewan. I blew it clean off. Just remember, holy water weakens a vampire, then they must be decapitated. A stake through the heart does not work. Save that stuff for the movies.

The Dusk Akers Family
Susie

She's mute and extremely pale. Her hair is almost white, and her eyes are light blue. She might be an albino vampire, but I don't know if that's possible.

THE DUSK AKERS
FAMILY

Zoe

Has blood orgies with her brothers Jordy and Arlo, and you didn't read that wrong. I told you this family is twisted and disturbing.

THE DUSK AKERS FAMILY

RUBY

THIS IS an anomaly of the group. They are overly mean to her and, from what I can tell, use her as a house servant. She cleans and takes care of the wounded. I don't feel sorry for her. If I see her, she's dead.

THE DUSK AKERS
FAMILY
JORDY

THIS ONE LIKES to kidnap and play with his food. He used to hunt near New River Gorge on bridge day. He'd take tourists and keep them for days before the family descends on the victim and drains them dry.

THE DUSK AKERS
FAMILY
ARLO

THE BABY OF THE BUNCH, the early twenties, maybe? I don't know much about him. Wally's notes don't mention him, so he must be a fresh face in the family.

THE DUSK AKERS FAMILY

EZRA*

I KILLED EZRA IN ROMNEY, West Virginia. He died alone, begging for his life in an alley after I dumped water blessed by Father McMillian and cut his head off. It's more than he deserved. Ezra was notorious for his barbaric nature. The rest should be easy now that I took out their powerhouse.

THE DUSK AKERS
FAMILY
MINNIE *

SHE TRIED to exact revenge for Ezra by coming to Wally's property at night while I slept. Jennifer and Timber were there, making this a terrible idea. I knew her movements before she did. I taunted her before I took her head. I made sure to let her know how Ezra died whimpering. The hate in her eyes when I killed her has been the most satisfying experience of this thing so far.

TIMBER

.

SPEAKING OF TIMBER, do not hurt him. If I am gone, and you are reading this, Timber is my dog. He is a two-year-old German Shepard who is hyper-intelligent. His IQ lands somewhere in the 125 range, according to Doctor Jeffery. He can not speak because he lacks vocal cords, but he knows what you are saying and communicates with nudges, barks, and pointing. Timber has saved my life numerous times, can see spirits, and has a sixth sense of danger.

Timber needs human blood to survive, type A, to be exact. The fridge in the garage is stored with blood at 42 degrees. It has to be thrown out if not used in 60 days. He eats in the morning and evening, mix a pack with his Alpo can, and he's fine. Doctor Jeffery gets the blood for me and has strict orders to get it for whoever takes Timber in if something happens to me.

GREEN BANK GLOW

GREEN BANK IS the home of many people who claim to suffer from electromagnetic hypersensitivity. It is a national quiet zone with no cell service or radio transmissions. They have a "radio cop" who enforces this, and his name is Zack Gardner. On the full moon, Zack strips naked and stands up near the dish. He mutters unintelligible phrases and is in an apparent trance. His entire body glows a fluorescent green. It could be aliens. After seeing the things I have, I can easily understand it, but I'm listing it as a monster for now.

BAD TOUCH BRAD

THIS ONE IS ANOTHER TRAGEDY. Much like FloraKate (I hate that name, but Jennifer is so proud of these.) Brad Dunfee lives in Bozoo and can not touch people. When he does, they are inflicted with what I can best describe as bad luck. It can be cancer, an auto accident, financial ruin, or worse. It has to be skin-on-skin. Even the slightest brush of his fingertips against you, and it happens. He cut his hands off in desperation to break the cycle. The in-home nurse tending to his wound care touched one of his stumps, and almost instantaneously, her husband sent her a text message that he was leaving her for her sister. I figure a star is incoming. I think he may commit suicide.

SLATY FORK SLITHER

JENNIFER IS TERRIFIED of snakes and couldn't give this one a name. The Slaty Fork Slither is over eleven feet long and emerald, with a thick yellow stripe down its back. What makes it a monster? Why the two heads it sports and the eight fangs a piece in both mouths. I thought it lived in Sharps Cave, but Jennifer and I have been through it with a fine tooth comb. It kills humans even if it leans more towards dogs and other large-breed animals. I have its shed skin here in the collection. How the hell do I keep missing it?

DELBARTON DREAM

Nina Klien married at 16 when her boyfriend Dwayne got her pregnant. She lost the baby at five months due to him being a jealous shit who used his fists. She'd gotten a ride home from work from another man.

She stayed with him (Of course she did) and lived the dream until she woke up beside him with his body completely shredded in 2014. He was so butchered that a tattoo on his calf was the only way to identify him. She was taken into custody. No weapon in the house matched the wound patterns, and because of the violence he inflicted on her the night before in a drunken stupor, she was still suffering the effects of a grade 3 concussion. There was no blood splatter on her body and a visceral trail led from Dwayne to the outside of their trailer.

Add all that to the fact he'd damned near killed her five or so times in the past, and the whole town turned a blind eye to it. No one wanted to see Nina convicted of this crime, and no one believed she did it. They all thought it impossible that she could have done something that insane and with such ferocity.

Nina told close personal friends, the sheriff, and a court-appointed psychologist that she dreamed a monster killed Dwayne. It looked like her but with elongated arms and hollowed-out eyes.

I wouldn't have taken much stock in that if it wasn't for the fact Nina was in a car accident that left her in a coma last year, and every full moon, she has a massive spike in brain activity. The next day, we have a body in a 25-mile radius. They are starting to pile up, murdered in the same manner Dwayne was.

FRIENDLY FOUR
TAMMY

FRIENDLY, West Virginia, is home to these four women. I want to say they are sisters, but records show different parents for each one. I'm not buying it. There are a lot of ghosts in the state, but 99 percent of them are harmless. These ladies can do reverse possession. They pull a spirit into their body. They take their memories and voice inflection while retaining a semblance of themselves. Tammy does it for profit. She charges for someone to talk to a dead relative. She's made a lot of money for it, sometimes giving people peace. She doesn't bother me in the slightest.

FRIENDLY FOUR
TERRY

TERRY DOES it for the thrill. She told me it was an unbelievable rush, the most unbelievable high she's ever felt. She keeps their memories. She tells me that they shouldn't be forgotten. It all sounds like a bunch of crazy hippie shit to me.

FRIENDLY FOUR
TRACY

TRACY IS where the apple starts to rot slightly. She takes their memories but uses the knowledge to hurt the living. A good example is a dead husband who kept his unfaithfulness from his wife. She goes and tells the grieving widow. All the while, the spirit witnesses it. It's pretty cruel.

FRIENDLY FOUR
TINA

TINA IS A SHITBAG. She takes the soul in and somehow dissipates it. She destroys it. I found her journal that described how she can feel them dying and how it brings her joy. She's on the run. I've tried to catch her, but it's hard without Jennifer's eyes. I can't risk Tina taking her.

ROB

TO THE NORTH side of Canaan Valley lives Rob, Bob's (#16) brother. He's no Bob. His fur is much lighter, almost gray. I've had to have him patched up several times after being shot, and I've had to deal with many different people who have seen him. Rob isn't aggressive, but he does go near humans. He isn't afraid of them and will certainly let loose on someone he feels is a threat. Rob loves the colder environments of our state and goes from Snow Shoe through Canaan Valley, but most of the time, I see him out there. I still wonder how they hide.

THE LONG RIDE

CHANDLER PIERCE WAS on his deathbed in 1999. His brother was at his side. The cancer had eaten Chandler through, and it was over. He begins asking his brother if he remembered how, in 1972, he called his brother and asked him to skip work to come home. Chandler's brother did, and that night, an accident at INCO Alloys killed three men in his department, including the man who replaced Chandler's brother for the evening.

Chandler then told how he'd been an awful man because his brother died. Rape, murder, and theft were nothing for him because he had no one to keep him in line after his brother passed. The odd thing about his story was none of that happened.

He then told his brother that in Cabell County, out McComas Road is a 1957 Chevy two-tone in blue and white, and its windows are completely tinted.

It roams the road and picks up a passenger, and the hooded driver gives them a chance to change one event in their life. Chandler says he took the long ride. He told his brother that the things it made him do were terrible but worth it for a second chance.

When asked what the driver made him do, Chandler took his last breath.

Chandler isn't the only person who has told a similar story. It has become West Virginia folklore. So much so that people roam McComas Road late at night, hoping to be picked up for a do-over.

COUNT IDIOT

THIS MAN LIVES OUTSIDE of Petersburg, West Virginia, and is a complete moron. He claims to have been born in 1501 in Romania and perished in the late 1550s of the flu. He told me his bones were brought here and buried in the soil outside of Petersburg, and he was resurrected. He dresses like Bela Lugosi and speaks like him, too. His home is adorned with gothic paintings and items from the 1700s, so he didn't do his homework.

I wouldn't have believed him if he hadn't slit his throat in front of me and didn't bleed. I watched as the wound closed. The one thing I've learned about West Virginia is that nothing comes for free. I wonder what this prick had to do to be like this. I do know he's not a vampire. I just hope it's not something worse.

WHOLLY TREE

SOMETHING LIVES inside a tree in Duck a few miles northeast of Clay, West Virginia. It's big, and no one can tell me what type of tree it is. There are a few holes in it, and people come from all over the state to reach within them. There is nothing 8 out of 10 times, and the person moves on feeling suckered for believing the rumors. Rarely, and I mean rarely, something is thrust into your hand worth more than your wildest dreams. It is maybe winning lottery numbers or a Spanish gold coin worth a hundred times its original price. Even rarer is that you get bit; if you do, God help you. It is the flesh-eating disease on steroids. You're dead in days, and the victims suffer.

The last person bit was 2024, so I finally went to see the tree. A young man named Andrew was out there chastising it and cursing up a storm. He then removed his belt and struck the tree several times, and I could have sworn I heard it cry.

I tried to ask him about what had just happened, and he told me to go fuck myself.

MUMBLES

Is Grace's cat and might be the most sought-after thing on this list. The reason my phone and radio went down the morning I met Grace? Mumbles, the familiar, is a good luck charm. #3 told me that he was blessed by the Goddess, which made my eyes roll. I don't have time for her hippie junk. In the wrong hands, Mumbles could cause a lot of destruction. I offered to help find him in exchange for whatever the witches were doing in Weirton they put on pause.

DETECTOR DIANA

DIANA VICKERS IS one of my favorite people in this mess. She can touch your skin and tell if you're lying or not. If you are dishonest about anything Diana knows, she has a great personality and is incredibly attractive. If Diana uses her gift, it takes a day off her life. I've never asked her to do it. She finds out about things and comes to me, offering to help. I hate it when she does it. It is so draining that she sometimes vomits or passes out shortly after. I try to visit her whenever I head to Blandville.

THE HANGING JUDGE

THIS HAPPENS MOSTLY in prisons in the state, so no one thought anything of it. I have two videos of the Judge dissing out punishment. A thin African American in a judicial black robe enters the cell of a convicted criminal on death row and hangs the victim. They don't fight back or argue; they seem to accept their fate. The rope he uses seems to be pulled from thin air. I would call him a ghost, but he has been filmed and seen by guards and other inmates. That's not how that works. The lights flicker, and he is just there. This isn't a priority right now. I have so many prison suicide files I'd have to start pouring over, and I don't have the time with the other pressing oddities.

THE ONA SCRAWL

A YOUNG WOMAN FROM ONA; when I ask her name, she tells me a different one each time. I have her prints, but nothing came back on them. She has so many things going on through her head. Talking to her is beyond confusing. It's as if she has a million stories in her mind trying to escape at once. If someone gives her a pen and paper, she starts writing about someone's death. At that exact moment, whatever she is writing about is happening. It's never anything happy or sweet; it's always tragic. Is she seeing this stuff, or is the terrifying part that she is causing it?

OPIE

THE OPIOID CRISIS ravaged this state. When I was an officer, I can't tell you how many people I dealt with who were committing crimes because of addiction. Jennifer would tell me stories of children abused and abandoned by parents who lived for fentanyl or heroin. We don't know this person's name, but Jennifer coined the nickname Opie in a brainstorming session. Opie preys on the addicted and gives them their "fix." Once they use it, he has control, and he uses them for all kinds of nefarious reasons, and before you say, well, that's all dealers. No, this is different. They have zero independent thought at all. They are mindless zombies that will commit murder, theft, rape, anything he wants.

They aren't after drugs anymore. They only serve him until he runs them dry. They don't eat, sleep, anything. They are completely and utterly in servitude.

Soap Opera Sarah

As Jennifer and I have written these down, we've realized many of West Virginia's monsters are human, or what passes as one. There are so many of them that just do horrible things. Take Sarah, for example; she approaches someone and stares into their eyes. This goes beyond simple amnesia. She takes everything from them, and most people inflicted die. It's like they are newborns again. Everything they have retained goes away forever. All sense of self disappears. I've interviewed one person who relearned their life, which took a decade. I wonder why someone would do this. I've got a photo of Sarah, she looks young. I'll get her. There are only so many places in this state to hide.

SYLVESTER SHADE

ANOTHER TRAGEDY; I hate these. I really do feel sorry for the people who can't help themselves. Holly Ramey lives in Sylvester and stays in a room devoid of light. Holly is only seventeen, and like most teenagers, her life is filled with anxiety. When she gets anxious, her shadow does whatever it wants. I don't understand it at all, but I know that it strangled a person; it's what started everything. Holly was with a young boy when she was fifteen, and when they went to be intimate, the shadow attacked him. (Maybe it saw him as a threat?) It moves across the wall and can reach out. I've seen it open and close doors. A doctor from Marshall University was studying her; his name escapes me now, but there was a ton of footage. During one of their sessions, the shadow entered his body and ripped him apart. She stays in the room alone in complete darkness. I know there is no cure for any of this except death, and that's so unfair.

CRANESVILLE CREEPER*

HOW MANY PEOPLE have died from this thing? This one I was proud of. Cranesville Swamp extends into Maryland, so I had a limited area to just West Virginia. The Creeper was covered in quacker moss. Jennifer calls it bog moss. It was a six-foot worm with teeth in a circle at its front that I assume was its mouth. It would stay in the wettest and coldest areas of the Swamp and hunt. Unbelievably silent and quick to devour its prey, its digestion is slow, and it remains beneath the water when full. Doctor Jefferey told me that certain earthworms can get close to the Creeper in length but nowhere this big in circumference. It was as big around as a grown man's thigh.

Doctor Jeffery is still mad at me because I burnt the bastard up, Timber, and I hunted it and wasn't taking any chances. We chased it on land, covered it in salt, and with a well-placed Molotov, it went quickly. I get that he wants to examine these things, but I would rather stay alive.

SALTY BOY

OUT IN SALT ROCK in the early 1990s, a man named Dale Lock beat his son Dale Jr. to death in a rage over his report card. He buried the body out in the woods. Senior and his wife made national headlines trying to "find" the boy. Everyone was looking for him, and the media descended on the tiny town, making hourly reports. The kid came back, though, and murdered his parents. Usually, I'd call that a win, but Junior never went back in the ground. Salty is a skeletal boy who has roamed the woods and town at night since 1991. I have no problem with him, but lately, he has been seen watching children playing at the school playground and staring at windows. I will have to talk with him if this doesn't stop. Even if the people of Salt Rock don't mind, it's getting unnerving.

BLACKWATER
BLOODSUCKER

THIS ONE, wow, this one. Blackwater Falls is home to a bat. Now, the largest bats in the world can get up to 13 inches from nose to tail. The one in Blackwater is 5, not inches, mind you, feet. He's (And it is he, according to Doctor Jeffery) entirely black with a white stripe down its back. It has killed people before. It has migrated from Smoke Hole Caverns to Blackwater Falls. Now, gigantic bats are one thing, but the rumor is that this is a curse placed upon Waitman T. Wiley, and this bat is his son, John.

Blackwater has no natural cave system for this bat to hide in. I think someone is housing this thing. Someone has to be taking care of it. Probably funded by the taxpayer, too; considering most of our politicians are aware of the bullshit that happens in this state, it wouldn't surprise me at all.

Mirror Max

THERE HAS BEEN a slight uptick in parricide lately. It would go unnoticed if not for some clever detective work on my part. In newly broken homes, mostly divorced, young children see a man in the mirror in the bathroom; he speaks to them and gets in their heads. He talks to them for months. The parent usually takes the child to a psychologist or scolds them for having an imaginary friend. Somehow, he convinces the kids that the parent is going to hurt them and tells them how to kill their parent creatively. He calls himself Max, and the three kids I've interviewed tell me he looks like a living cartoon. I have no idea what that means. Could he be animated? He seems only to affect the towns of Pendleton County. I'll start my investigation there.

Sloppy Suttons*

Sutton had a lovely nursing home called Almost Heaven. It was quite large and housed probably 35 elderly people. Mays called me to investigate family members claiming they were "doing" something to their loved ones. Saying they weren't themselves and overly "nice." Timber went wild when we arrived, and Jennifer could tell something was off. Upon investigation, all the staff and patients turned on us before melding together into a giant glob of flesh with arms, legs, and eyes.

Using Jennifer to see around corners and cutting the power trapping it in the recreation room. (Thank God for electronic locks.) We set the facility ablaze, killing it inside. There was no news report, and I've not heard a soul mention it. How far can the cover-ups in this state go?

.

Paw Paw Piper

Paw Paw, West Virginia, has one of the worst problems I've encountered while trying to stop the monsters. Located in Morgan County and only having a population of over 400, no one who calls it home can leave. While visiting, I noticed a lot of long faces and could see the pain in their eyes. I understood when the men at the gas station broke out in song and dance. Something is controlling the residents here, and it turns into a perverse musical number every so often.

I've witnessed it, the singing of their conversations warning you to run away, claiming that "He" could make you dance yourself to death. It was during a chorus of "Please God shoot me, make it stop" that I swore to avenge those afflicted somehow. I don't know who is responsible, and I'm afraid to stay there too long. The one question that keeps me up at night is, where does the music come from?

PHINEAS

I AM to stay far away from Phineas, a giant man with only the whites of his eyes. There are no pupils, and he dresses like something from the Victorian era of history. He spoke in a British accent, and when we talked, he was overly polite, even if he had the most unnatural smile. Mays told me to avoid Phineas at all costs and that Officer Oakley was the only one skilled enough to handle him. He warned that I had no idea the power Phineas wielded and to run in the other direction if I saw him approach. Mays was adamant about it and claimed he wouldn't go within 100 yards of the creature. I have a frightening suspicion that Phineas might be the Devil.

Fairview Fielder *

Jennifer again getting cute with her names. I don't understand why she didn't just call it the Fairview Scarecrow. It doesn't matter now it's dead. I don't know if it was brought to life by a curse, but this here has the prestigious honor of being the first real monster Jennifer and I went after together after she fought Nothing to the death. I shot the Fielder (So stupid) in the chest with a Mossberg 12 gauge, and a human heart spilled out onto the dirt. I ran over it with a hay baler and tossed pieces in separate parts of the state. I haven't heard anything about disappearing residents in Fairview since. I think we got him

LEWIS COUNTY
LIZARD MAN

I DON'T KNOW if the lizard people story started from this because someone talked, but the Mayor of Weston, West Virginia, is a lizard. Yes, he wears a skin suit, and his name is Chris. He is beloved by the city and owns a laundromat that he doesn't charge the less fortunate to use. Chris is a little too good to be true. He's too pleasant and way too sociable to be what he is. He has a wife named Tiffany, who is not a lizard person, mind you, and NO, I don't know if they are intimate. I do know that they have no children, and I have no idea what a humanoid reptile penis would look like. But I know that Jennifer has begged me to send her off on a "scouting mission." I can't spare her right now. I need her with me.

There are no unexplained disappearances or instances of foul play in Weston, so I will let it go for now. But Chris is aware of me and commented that I'm doing the Lord's work. I just know this bastard is shady; I don't know how.

THE OUTLAW OF
KNOB FORK

THE DAVIS GANG was a real threat to the area back in 1888. One of those outlaws was a man named Grover McKinney. He was the oldest of the gang and didn't like the whole killing part. He loved the money and the easiest way to get it was by robbing stagecoaches and people traveling to bigger towns. One day, they happened upon a coach that held two young women inside, and one of the gang members thought he'd take a little more than her brooch.

Grover didn't take too kindly to it, and low and behold, he got a bullet in his chest for his trouble. He was buried in a shallow grave along with the two women the members of the gang murdered. They'd got what they wanted and had one less person to split the spoils with.

Grover stayed in the ground for about a year. The only thing I can come up with is that another monster was killed, and the state chose him. He emerged from the earth and killed every one of them, and he's roamed the woods near Knob Fork ever since. The people give him a wide berth and don't approach him. I don't know what to do about him. Wally's notes claim he is harmless and wants to be left alone. There have been no stories of him hurting anyone since returning, so I don't know. I may have to try and talk to him.

THE BURNT HOUSE DRAGON

BURNT HOUSE IS a small community out in Ritchie County, and no, I am not making the name up. You've read that right, too; a dragon is out there. He is three feet in length and a pet of a young boy whose nickname is Muff. When I read this back, I want to get in my car and get out of here. Muff, which I learned on my last visit is short for Muffin, found the egg in a creek bed and has been raising the animal since it hatched three years ago. He even named it, and as stupid as it sounds, he named it Dragon. I'm starting to worry because it's growing and gone from its regular diet of candy bars and Mountain Dew to rats and rabbits.

It loves Muff (I realized it after I wrote it, shut up.). It is very protective of the boy and won't leave his side. It also has razor-sharp claws and a nasty row of teeth. It doesn't put me at ease when it breathes fire, either. I'm going to have to do something.

Clovis the Clown

JENNIFER IS AFRAID OF CLOWNS. She fought a demon from hell and killed it. Yet lives in mortal terror of clowns. So I can't use her on this, even knowing Clovis can't see her. This one falls to Timber and me. Clovis Farley was a mechanic in the 1940s from the town of Hamlin. A jolly man loved by all who knew him, Clovis gave no one around him reason to suspect he was a monster before he became one. Clovis played the part of Santa at a small store for the kids during Christmas, and in the summer, he dressed up as a clown for the town festival. The photos included don't do it justice. He was a mountain of a man; the clown garb in the first picture is what he wore, the yellow and red.

I don't know how any child could find his look funny, but it was a different time. Clovis held a secret, though. He would go to other towns to widows' homes. He would don his outfit and break in, torturing them to death. I have no idea if he sexually assaulted them. They didn't test for that, but the crime scene descriptions are horrific. Some of his victims were over the age of seventy-five. Clovis was killed in 1948. A lot of rumors and innuendo state it was mob justice. That he was found out, and I believe that.

The problem is that widow killings keep happening much less frequently, but they still occur. There have been sightings of a clown matching these descriptions near the vicinity of victims as late as 2022. I know it's him. I can feel it.

QUEEN STING

THERE IS a twelve-inch long yellow jacket near Romance, West Virginia. She stings you, you're paralyzed, and once you are, she tears into her prey and consumes their blood. This queen usually leaves them drained dry. It wasn't until Doctor Jeffery and I spoke about it that he figured out that her victims had high glucose levels in their bloodstream. I've searched for her and can't find her. I need a different strategy here. I hope to Christ there's not a nest of them.

TINKER TOY BUILDER

I DON'T WANT to call Luzuriaga (I don't know his first name) a monster, but it can be easily abused in a situation like this. Luz, as I affectionately call him, lives in a house near Indian Mills. When you walk through the door, you are greeted by all these fantastic wooden toys he makes. Everything is crafted in such high quality and exquisite the old saying is that they don't make them that way anymore.

Because they don't, you enter the house in 2025, but inside, it is 1945, and the war has just ended. If Luz leaves his home, it is 1945, but somehow, there is a loop here where anyone who comes to the door in this current year can enter his world. Whenever they leave the house, they are back in 2025, so that's not the issue. What if someone starts telling him things to come, and he changes the future? Or what if someone brings him technology that the people of the 1940s shouldn't have?

Luz is a sweetheart, but the consequences of one slip-up would be catastrophic. I don't need any butterfly effect bullshit happening because someone let him see their phone. At least the State Police watch his house night and day for visitors.

.

SNOW SCREAM

CALHOUN COUNTY IS one of my favorite places in West Virginia. My grandmother and I always went to the Wood Festival. I know it for a different reason as an adult: I hate the winter months because when the snow falls in Calhoun, schools close instantly, and all local businesses shut their doors. If the snow gets above 4 inches, it does many times over. A moving pile of snow will go on the hunt. It doesn't look like a snowman, but more like a pile where someone has shoveled or a small drift, and if it grabs you, it takes seconds to devour you. It leaves nothing but a blood stain smattering through the white. I have no idea how to track it.

CHURCH OF THE ENAMEL

I DON'T WANT to call him a reverend, but he claims he is one. Dale Allen is the leader of a disturbing tiny church in Peewee. He had about fifty members from all over the state, which is growing alarmingly. His parish offers their teeth to him, scattered across the stage and pulpit. He gives his followers alcohol, which he calls the blood of the receiver, and then pulls their teeth with pliers. We know he's doing this, but no one will come forward and say he took their teeth. He keeps babbling on about the receiver and that he lives in the woods, ready to take their offering and more. Why am I mentioning this as a monster and not just a fucking wack job?

Four miles outside of the church's grounds near a small family cemetery, one of theirs was found dead with all of their bones removed. There were no incision marks. The skeleton was completely gone, as if pulled out the mouth. I'm starting to think the receiver is real, and I need to find out what we are dealing with.

Blood Boom

Apple Grove is home to a very peculiar set of leeches. They are pretty tiny and don't grow when they feed. Suppose you were to get one on you. It would seem normal until you try to get it off. A form of defense mechanism kicks in, and it injects a substance through its anterior sucker. This causes the host's head to explode. They are mainly in a creek bed out Horse Creek Road, and the folks there avoid them, but still. I have a vial of the stuff to deliver to the good doctor to analyze when I get a chance.

COWENSTEIN

SOME PRICKS' idea of a cute little joke: We had to pick up a cow from Mercer County that has been stitched together from other cow parts. I've had to keep it away from prying eyes at Wally's (My house now). It's alive somehow, and Dr. Jefferey had attempted to euthanize it several times to no avail. How did they accomplish this? Who did this? Why did they do this? The one question I have is if her udders look full. What is in there? There is no way in hell I am going to find out.

VECTOR GIRL

I HAD no idea what vector graphics were after Jennifer described this. This child, maybe 2 or 3 years old, appeared in a home in Taylor County. A young man named Tommy was getting ready for work when she came out of a dark corner. He described her as something made like a video game. I thought of something cartoonish, but he meant something like Asteroids. A shaky glowing green outline, nothing but an even darker green inside. She asked for candy, and he just happened to be eating a Charleston Chew and gave it to her. He watched her consume it and then fade away into where she came from.

It happened several weeks later at another home three miles away. Lana Simmons was in her kitchen when the girl appeared behind her asking for a grilled cheese sandwich. Lana did what was asked of her. After handing the food to her, the kid scarfed it down and noticed Lana was crying. Vector Girl looked at her and told her it was, "It's okay, you gave me what I wanted." before fading out again. Alright, so what happens when she doesn't get what she wants?

FLOOD LIGHT

PIKESIDE AT NIGHT after a storm can be dangerous. It's so close to Martinsburg, which has a pretty high population. There have been a few random incidents, but people are starting to ask questions, so I will investigate it before the end of the month. Three males of vastly different ages have been outside working or getting in their vehicle when they saw a bright light close to them. When they turn to inspect it, they almost fall into a trance. One of the men describes it as a pulsing blue light. The other said it was pink.

Either way, all three stared at it, and it fried their retinas. The men are now blind, and it's permanent. In each instance, the men are discovered naked, so it takes the victim's clothing. Rape kits have been done, and there has been no evidence of sexual assault or the like.

GOVENOR'S BALL

CLARENCE MEADOWS SERVED as the state's governor from 1945 to 1949. A lot of things I have looked up about the man say that he was friendly, kind, and at one point, was going to make a damn fine preacher. This was a good man; typically, when you hear the phrase honest politician you'd scoff, but Meadows was the real deal. He was also the first to investigate the crazy shit that happened in this state. He even created a task force to put these creatures down at the time. After zero luck in stopping anything, he disbanded it, and after his term ended, he moved to Florida and left us behind. Or that is how the story goes.

His task force was quite competent, and after a successful mission, he had brought some artifacts, and one of those happened to be a cast iron mill ball about 4 inches big with strange small writing on it.

In his curiosity and being a man of several degrees (mostly in law) and a scholar, Governor Meadows attempted to translate the text and, to my surprise, was successful. After he read it aloud, the four men in the room complained of it getting extremely hot before they melted in front of him. The ball was a warning, and the message was loud and clear. Someone wanted the Governor to back off, and he did. He always blamed himself for those men's deaths, and his diary (Which is in here somewhere.) talks about wanting revenge on whoever tricked him. My money is on Phineas, but that's not the scary part. The ball used to be in this room with the rest of the relics and is missing. I didn't take it out of here, so someone has been rummaging through here, and it is the only thing gone.

Lady of the Night

I HAVE no idea how long this has been going on, but no one would know if it weren't for dinner between colleagues. Several men across the state have been having dreams. They all start the same way. A mousy woman with glasses comes to them and starts a conversation before it becomes violent and sexual, with the men not able to fight back or refuse. The men would wake feeling drained and disturbed by it. Then, it would happen again the following night and the next.

Eventually, the men didn't want to sleep, it is too emotionally draining. The men are all the same type: successful in their fields, in great shape, and single. The trauma on these men led them to psychologists who would prescribe Prazosin. It didn't help these attacks would continue until the victims died of lack of sleep, two from accidents related to it, one from a heart attack, and another who sadly took his own life.

The dinner between the doctors led to them discussing the case, and to each of their dismays, they were all patients that met this fate. The scary part is that the woman they described is the same person. Two of those affected were capable artists and drew her. It's her, and I wonder how many men she's done this to that never came forward?

Something

PLEASE DON'T BE what I think this is; two months ago, Mays and Oakley brought me a report of a woman butchered by a tall creature that leaned to one side, had long claws, and was covered in blood. The last thing on the sheet they handed me was her interview. She said that it didn't have eyes. Let this just be something else, something similar. God, please don't be him. Don't let him be back.

Made in the USA
Columbia, SC
21 September 2024

42718240R00071